Note to Parents

All pre-school children love looking at animals, imitating their sounds and learning about their homes and routines, so this book will provide hours of fun. The playful story and irresistible cast of farm animals will delight the very youngest child, whilst older children will be fascinated by the abundant detail on every page.

This book offers a wealth of early learning experiences. Talk about the story to develop your child's vocabulary and encourage verbal fluency. Draw attention to familiar words to instil confidence with the idea of printed language. Discuss the details in the pictures to develop observational skills – which will be important later for learning to read – and play the games at the end of the book to reinforce these skills and introduce new ones.

Little Rabbits' First Farm Book also offers an excellent way to introduce your child to life beyond the home and broaden their experience of the outside world. In our increasingly urban society it is more important than ever to appreciate how nature affects our everyday lives, since by understanding our environment we can protect it. Discovering how animals are reared and how food is grown will help your child to develop an affinity with the natural world and an interest in preserving it for the future. Above all, learning about the farm is fun – so delight in your child's excitement as they find out more about the world around them.

The Publisher wishes to thank Jill Clay, Education Consultant to the National Union of Farmers, for her kind assistance in the development of this book.

KINGFISHER
An imprint of Kingfisher Publications Plc
New Penderel House, 283-288 High Holborn
London WC1V 7HZ

First published by Kingfisher 2001
2 4 6 8 10 9 7 5 3 1
ITR/0401/TWP/FR/170ARM

Text and illustrations copyright © Alan Baker 2001

A CIP catalogue record for this book is available from the British Library.

ISBN 0 7534 0574 1

Printed in Singapore

Little Rabbits'
First Farm Book

Alan Baker

KINGFISHER

Wake up, farm!

It's early in the morning and the Little Rabbits have come to help on the farm.
The cockerel is crowing.

Cock-a-doodle-doo!

Time for all the animals to wake up!

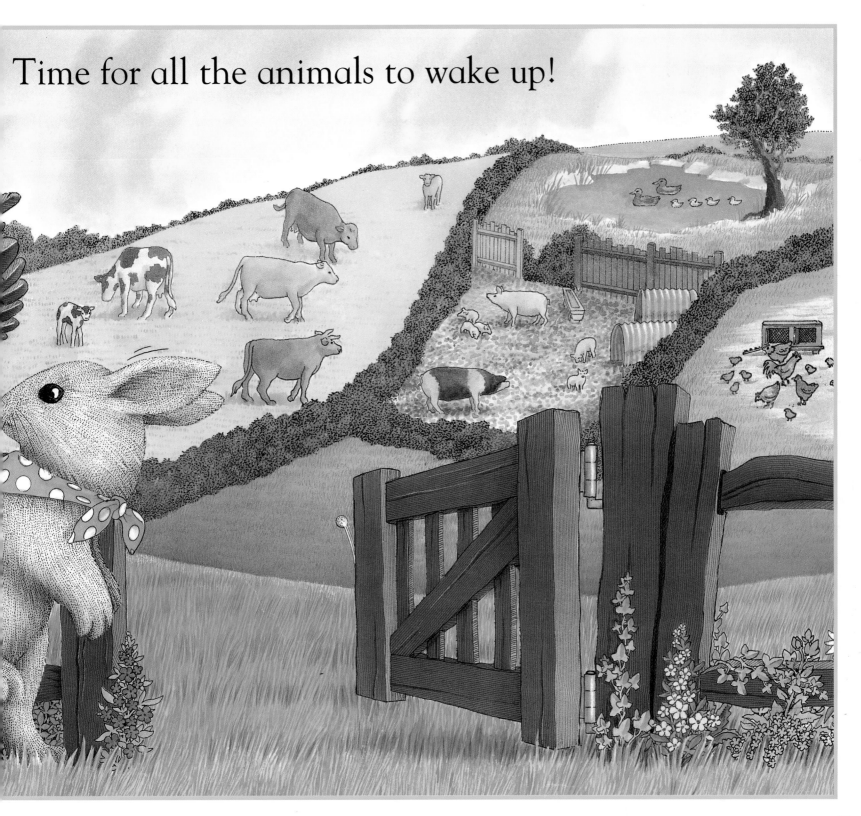

Chickens clucking

The hens and the chicks are first to be fed.
Black and White Rabbit gives them corn to eat.
Grey Rabbit collects the eggs from the hen house.

Cluck!
Cluck!

Did You Know?

Hens can lay eggs every day.
Look what eggs are used for:

Animal Families

Cockerel

Hen

Chick

Ducks quacking

Brown Rabbit is feeding the ducks.
The fluffy ducklings are swimming in the pond.
Don't fall in the water, Brown Rabbit!

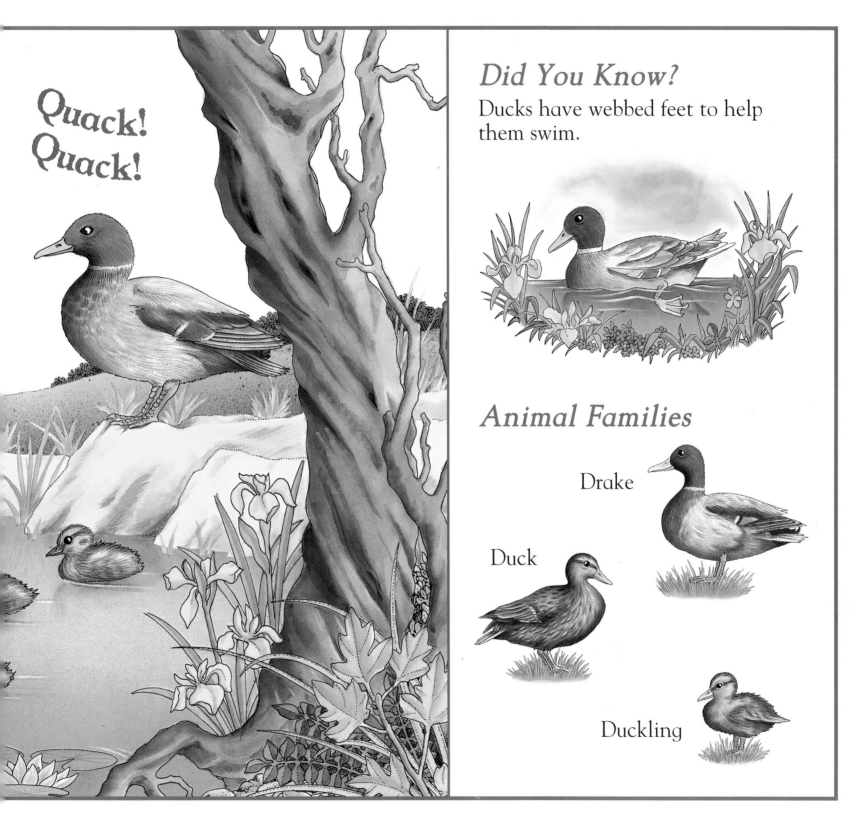

Quack!
Quack!

Did You Know?

Ducks have webbed feet to help them swim.

Animal Families

Drake

Duck

Duckling

Cattle moo-ing

The bull and the cow are ready for breakfast.
Here comes Grey Rabbit with some hay for them.
Look who is feeding the new calf!

Moo! Moo!

Did You Know?

Cows eat grass to make milk. Hay is dried grass.

Milk comes out of the cow's udder.

Animal Families

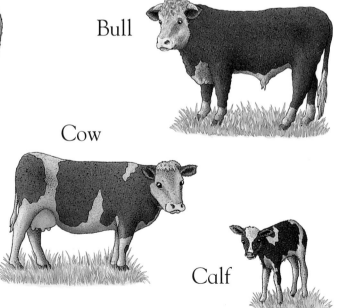

Bull

Cow

Calf

Pigs oinking

The pigs and the piglets are hungry, too.
White Rabbit pours grain into the trough.
The piglets snuggle up to drink their milk.

Oink!
Oink!

Did You Know?

Pigs live in sties. They love to roll around in the mud. Mud protects them from the sun.

Animal Families

Boar

Sow

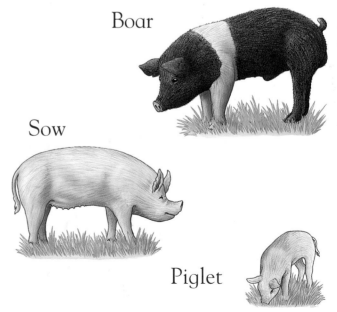

Piglet

Sheep baa-ing

Brown Rabbit is taking the sheep to a field where there is lots of juicy fresh grass to eat. Hurry up, little lambs!

Baa! Baa!

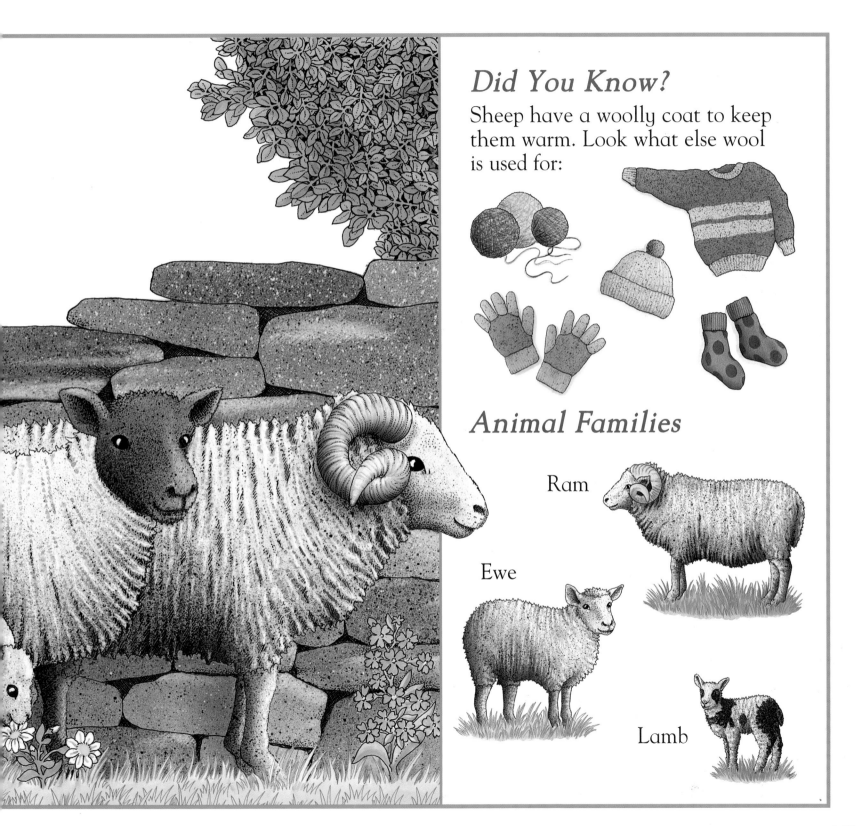

Did You Know?

Sheep have a woolly coat to keep them warm. Look what else wool is used for:

Animal Families

Ram

Ewe

Lamb

Tractor chugging

It's time to plant the seeds that will grow into wheat. White Rabbit drives the tractor across the field. What a lot of noise it makes!

Chug!
Chug!
Chug!

Did You Know?

Tractors pull machines called ploughs to dig up the ground and make it ready for planting.

Wheat gives us grain, which is made into flour.

Look what flour is used for:

Picking the apples

The apples in the orchard are ready for picking. Some are growing right at the top of the trees. Hold on tight, Black and White Rabbit!

Did You Know?

Lots of different fruits and vegetables are grown on the farm.

Look what apples are used for:

21

Milking the cows

Now it's time for the cows to be milked.
Brown Rabbit collects the milk in a pail.
Mind the swishy tail, White Rabbit!

Did You Know?

Cows are milked twice a day on the farm. Most are milked by a special machine.

A tanker takes the milk to the factory.

Look what milk is used for:

Let's go shopping

The farm shop sells food that comes from the farm.
Black and White Rabbit has a long shopping list.
What do you want for dinner, Little Rabbits?

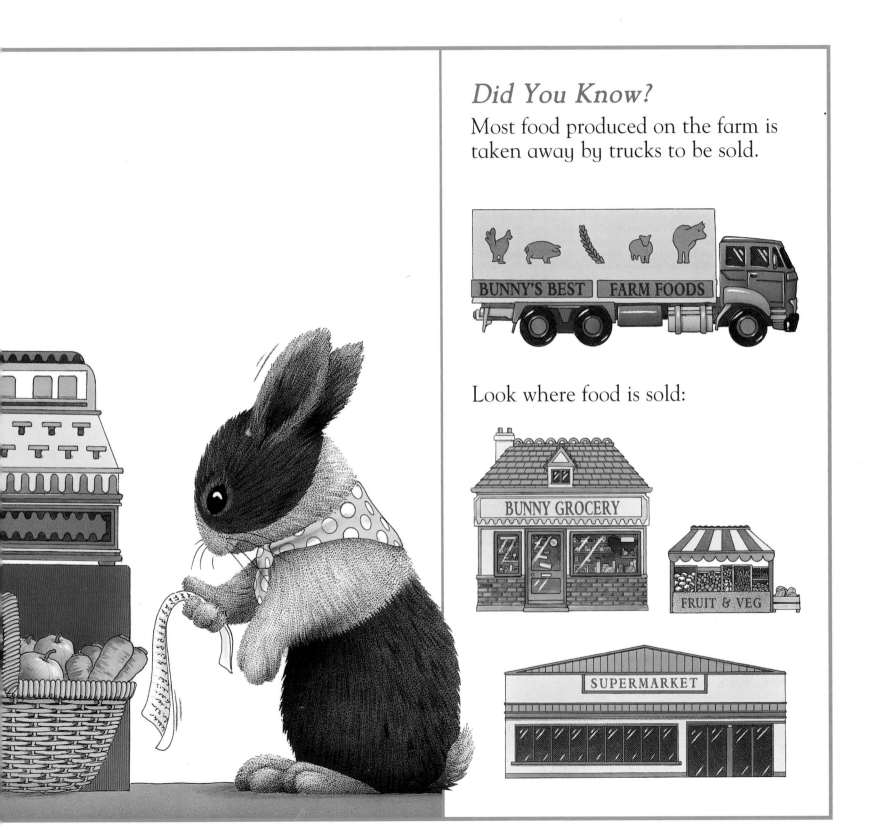

Did You Know?

Most food produced on the farm is taken away by trucks to be sold.

BUNNY'S BEST   FARM FOODS

Look where food is sold:

BUNNY GROCERY

FRUIT & VEG

SUPERMARKET

Goodnight, farm

It's late now and the Little Rabbits must go home.
Don't forget to shut the gate behind you!

Zzzz, zzzz!

Goodnight, farm.
Goodnight, Little Rabbits.

Games to play

Playing these games with your child will help them to develop observational, verbal and sorting skills. You will be building their understanding of the world around them and providing the foundation for early literacy and numeracy.

Names and noises

Children love identifying animals and imitating their sounds. Pointing to the pictures, ask your child to name each animal and to make the right animal sound. Alternatively, ask your child to point to the animal whose sound you make. Match the picture of each animal to its label to encourage recognition of these familiar words.

Mix and match

Does the cow live in the hen house? Does the pig live in the pond? Help your child to match each animal to its farmyard home.

All different kinds

Looking at colour, shape and pattern, help your child describe how the farm animals differ from one another – and in which ways they are similar. How many animals have two legs and how many have four? Extend and practise vocabulary by providing further detail with words such as fur, feathers, fleece and tail.

Where's Mouse?

Children adore the game of hide-and-seek. Ask your child to find the little brown mouse that appears throughout the book and help your child to describe what he is doing.

Food on the farm

Look at the food you have at home and talk to your child about how this came to be there. Which of the foods described in the book can they find in their refrigerator or store cupboard? You may decide to extend this to a discussion about foods not mentioned in the book but familiar to your own child – for example, animal products such as meat.

Day and night on the farm

Try this simple game of spot the difference. Look again at the opening pages 6 and 7 and the closing pages 26 and 27. What differences can your child identify between the two scenes? Use this as a basis for a discussion about time – day and night and early and late – and the routines associated with different times of the day.

Animals everywhere

boar

bull

calf

chick

cockerel

cow

drake

duck

duckling

ewe

hen

lamb

piglet

ram

sow

Now match the baby animals to their parents.